THE Ellie McDoodle DIARIES

New Kid in School

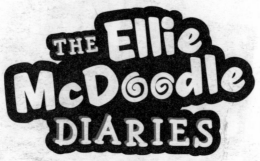

THE Ellie McDoodle DIARIES

by Ruth McNally Barshaw

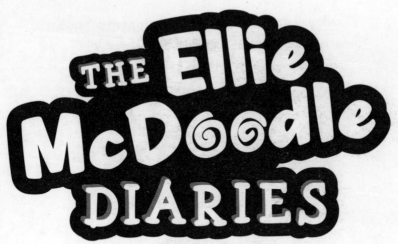

THE Ellie McDoodle DIARIES

New Kid in School

WRITTEN AND ILLUSTRATED BY

Ruth McNally Barshaw

BLOOMSBURY

LONDON   NEW DELHI   NEW YORK   SYDNEY

To Brenda, Marty, Jacque, and Jan

Thank you to the community of students, families, faculty, and staff of Attwood School for letting me observe and sketch them at work and at play.

Thank you to Peter Catalanotto for letting me mimic some of his art on p. 157.

Bloomsbury Publishing, London, New Delhi, New York and Sydney

First published in Great Britain in April 2014 by Bloomsbury Publishing Plc
50 Bedford Square, London WC1B 3DP

www.bloomsbury.com

Bloomsbury is a registered trademark of Bloomsbury Publishing Plc

First published in the USA in July 2008 by Bloomsbury Children's Books
1385 Broadway, New York, New York 10018

A CIP catalogue record for this book is available from the British Library

ISBN 978 1 4088 5596 6

MIX
Paper from
responsible sources
FSC® C020471
www.fsc.org

Printed and bound in Great Britain by CPI Group (UK) Ltd, Croydon CR0 4YY

1 3 5 7 9 10 8 6 4 2

The End.

Seriously. This is the end. I'm doing this new
journal to keep track of my family's move to a
new house (new city, new schools, new everything).
There won't be much to keep track of,
though, because this is the END
of everything good.

Ophelia, eating cereal

My house: Gone

We're moving away, and I probably won't ever see it again.

Good-bye, room.

Clouds painted by me and Mom when I was four

Good-bye, bird tree.

Grandpa made all these birdfeeders.
We get millions of birds.
How will they find our new house?
Will they starve?

Good-bye, four-leaf clover patch.

I found 27 four-leaf clovers, 6 five-leaf clovers, 2 six-leaf clovers, a seven, an eight, and a NINE, all in my own backyard. If we move, all the good luck stays here without us.

Good-bye, basement.
Dad used to play
old music and
dance with me
and Risa and Mom.
Who's going to
dance in my
basement when
we leave?

Dipping me.
I'm screaming
and laughing.

Good-bye, playroom in the attic.

When we were little, my cousin Deanna dropped
a tiny doll down the heating grate and we never
got it out.

It's still there!

All these things make this MY house. We can't
move. We can't abandon all these special things!
But we are. Everything is for sale. My memories,
my whole life—sold, to the highest bidder.

I don't want to believe we're actually moving, but all the signs point to it:
Mom's cranky . . .

. . . the living room is piled high with boxes. Mom used to have better decorating ideas than this.

Mom says you have a choice for dinner: cereal or a sandwich. Everything else is packed.

I want a tuna fish sandwich.

You can have one tomorrow at the new house. Today you get peanut butter.

Cheezers.

I've seen Josh and Dad in better moods.

Only Ben-Ben the monkey boy is happy. To him, it's all an adventure.

5

So this is really it.

Our last night in our house.

I'm packing my whole existence into a stack of cardboard boxes.

My sad face on the box means the box goes in my sad new room.

Moving Day.

My friends come over. I'm trying not to cry.

We're broken, permanently. We decide to create a group journal. Each person will take it for one week and write or draw in it. Then they'll pass it to the next person. I get it for the first week.

Then, just like that, my family says it's time to go.

Risa, me,
and Ophelia

Mom and
Ben-Ben

It feels like we're driving faster than we need to.

Zoom—we're on Main Street. Zoom—we're on the highway. Zoom—we're leaving behind every important thing: friends, home, sanity. Everything inside me screams to turn back, go back home. Maybe Risa is right and this sadness will end. I don't know. I've never felt so lost before. Everything is going downhill.

Dad and Josh

On the road 20 minutes:

The diesel exhaust from the moving vans is making me sick. My stomach is all knotted up and my throat feels like I tried to swallow a golf ball. I'll have to do something or I'll start crying again. Or worse.

I decide to work on the group journal. This is like a funeral.

My Bequests to Our Group:

To Aggy I leave my name, Ellie McDoodle, which she thought up three years ago because I doodle a lot.
To LaTasha I leave my happiness.
To Theo I leave my sense of humor.
To Kiki I leave my smile.
To Alex I leave my laugh.
To April I leave my jokes.

I won't need these things anymore.

I found this leaf near my house.

Good-bye to my house and neighborhood.

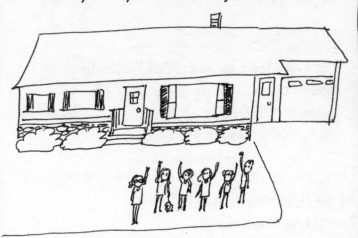

It's a two-hour drive to my new house. Nothing interesting to see—just the back of a moving van.

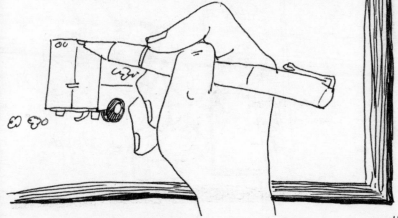

This is it.
The new house.

The yard has a lot of trees. But NO tire swings, and I don't see any four-leaf clovers.

The stairs look rickety.

Figures!

This isn't very inviting.
Everything is empty.
My voice bounces off the walls like Ben-Ben
on sugar.

No time to sit around. I have to help haul stuff.

I'm almost having fun until I remind myself
I don't want to be here and all my friends are
far away.

I have to share a room with my sister. My mom says Risa will go off to college in a year and then I'll have the room to myself. But Risa's pushing for me to share a room with Ben-Ben now instead!

(I decorated my boxes so I'd know what's inside.)

I am a worthless pawn, moved around by the real players of the game.

When I was little, I used to cry myself to sleep because in a weird way it felt good.

But I can't do that here. Risa will make fun of me, or Mom will give me a job to do.

Anyway, I've already cried and it isn't helping. My throat hurts and my nose is plugged and I can't breathe.

That's it—I'm suffocating in here. I have to get out.

Dad and Mom are returning the moving vans—now's my chance to slip out.

This book.

The sky is gray. It's windy. I can hear the leaves rustling. I hear a dog barking—it sounds like a BIG dog. It smells like it's going to rain.

Birds flying south.

They don't like living here.

No sidewalks here. No curbs, just gravel on the road.

What's over that hill?

My path: →   →   hill

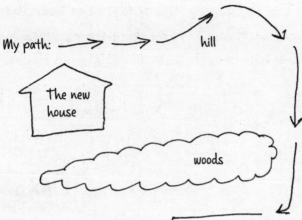

The new house

woods

Finally! Signs of life. It's a library.

This place is humongous!
The kids' books are upstairs. So far, so good . . .

I find the books
I like and get cozy.
It's not too quiet,
not too noisy. Lots
to look at. And
MILLIONS
of books.
I could
live here.

But wait!

And we talk about all the books I've read recently.

Finally, a plan. Read, and just ignore real life! There's some other kids here who look my age, but they're busy talking and I'm just fine sitting here reading. Miss Claire kept saying I should make myself comfortable, so I am.

I read for HOURS.

Miss Claire stops by a few times with suggestions of books for me. I even have a new library card! (I couldn't remember my new address, but Miss Claire said I could check out some books now and bring in my address tomorrow.)

I check out five books that seem to fit my life:

1) Boy crashes in Canadian wilderness and has
   to survive on his wits alone.

   > My life: girl stuck in strange
   > new wilderness has to survive on
   > her wits alone (plus books).

2) Boy has supernatural powers to help him
   fight evil.

   > My life: girl with NO powers has to
   > fight evil.

3) Girl starts at a new school and everyone
   hates her until partway through the
   school play.

   > My life: hmm, I hope this isn't telling
   > me the future—I can't act!

4) Girl loses important object and dies; after
   death she has to find the object.

   > My life: I'm lost AND I feel like I've
   > died. Cheezers.

5) Girl observes everything around her and
   keeps a journal about her misery.

   > My life: um, yeah.

Dinnertime; I should go.

Mom insists on dinner together as a family. Usually it's comic relief. Josh is in rare form tonight.

What do you put in the toaster?

A plane crashes right at the intersection of four states: Utah, New Mexico, Arizona, and Colorado. Where are the survivors buried?

We're all yelling out wrong answers.

Hold on there, sport.

Is anyone keeping score?

Two points for Josh!

Ben-Ben, no dribbling.*

The right answers to Josh's questions:
A. They both weigh the same.
B. A towel
C. An umbrella
D. Bread
E. Survivors aren't buried.

*Dad's a coach. He always talks in sports-speak.

25

What I Don't Like about Being Here:
(Where do I begin?)
1) Sharing a room with Risa. She keeps telling me to get out of her way, even though she actually spends a lot of time in the bathroom. Why can't she just sleep in there?
2) No friends. Except maybe Miss Claire.
3) Everything familiar is gone.
4) School is going to be awful. No, it'll be worse than that. It'll be horrible. Terrible. Catastrophic. Devastating. Excruciating.

Excruciating? You're describing how it is for me to share a room with you, right?

5) No privacy!

To keep us from killing each other, Mom takes us school shopping. Yippee.

These are huge.

They're perfect. You're going to grow a lot this year.

Mom, since I don't need new jeans, can we spend that money on jewelry instead?

But it gets worse . . .

I'm trying on shirts and pants. Risa wants to come in.

Too many people shopping, not enough dressing rooms.

Okay, I'm done.

See ya, Elmo.

I hate when she calls me Elmo.

I hate that she has such an easy time finding new clothes that fit.

Mom wants to buy me a skirt. I don't like skirts. They look stupid on me.

Why wasn't I born prettier?

Will I always have freckles?

Does Risa call me Elmo because I look like a boy?

Do striped toe socks go with sandals?

I'm reaching down to pull up my sock when someone opens the door on me.

Slam!

Oh! Some-one's in there!

Oh. My. GOSH. I hear laughing.

Did you see that girl in her underwear? Ha-ha!

I'm thinking about just giving up and dying of embarrassment when Mom knocks on the door.

Ellie?

Elmo!

"Butt," it's a good thing you have clean underwear on!

Ellie, come on out.

Elmo, nobody saw. Come on.

I don't care what we buy anymore. I just want to get to the car FAST.

Later, I can't sleep.

What if the kids who saw me go to my new school?
Risa keeps saying it's no big deal.
How can she even think that?
As soon as it's light outside, I head up to the library. Eventually the city wakes up.

Ellie! Good morning! How are you?

Hi, Miss Claire. I'm okay.

I have an idea to make myself feel better.

Family for Sale: Bid Often!

I show my ad to Miss Claire, who says she appreciates my humor. Then she asks me more about Ben-Ben. I tell her about his antics. Better yet, I show her. She sympathizes.

One time he aimed wrong and landed on my back. OUCH.

His favorite trick? Piling everything in my room into one very tall tower. Now that Risa and I are sharing a room, he piles all our stuff together. What a mess! But this gives me an idea. I exchange my books for some new ones and race home.

My Quest for a New Room:

This is ideal.
Mom says no.

An apartment in the living room? No.

Take over the hallway closet? No.

Funny, there's no room to hang my clothes.

The basement? Too dark, too cold, way too scary.

When I go downstairs I whistle really loud so if a monster grabs me, everyone upstairs will hear me stop whistling and they'll come down and investigate. (Okay, realistically I know that won't happen, but I get to make the rules in my nightmare.)

The attic?

This could be perfect!

Please, please can I have the attic for my bedroom?

Problems!

1) Mom thinks the attic is too dirty.

2) Dad can't help clean or move furniture because he's working on deadline stuff for his new job.

3) Risa's suddenly interested in the attic!

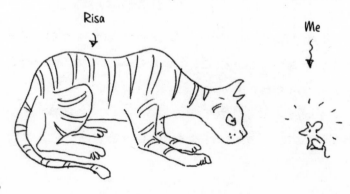

Risa

Me

How do I make the attic sound like a good idea to Mom but a bad idea to Risa? Even Josh comes to watch me squirm.

I give it absolutely every bit of logic, reasoning, and drama I can manage.

First, Risa:
☑ It's too far from the bathroom.
☑ What a lot of work to clean out the attic.
☑ The room Risa has now is cleaner, bigger, and could be a nice private space.

In the end, I convince Risa to stay in the room we share now. Success!

Then I convince Mom I'll work hard to clean the attic. Mop it, scrub it, polish it . . . And she says yes! I can move in! Dad says, "Do it right or it's game over." But I feel it's first down and goal. I'm really close to winning this!

39

Mrs. Claus
A two-foot-tall munchkin of malice.

waves a menacing candle

don't let this sickly sweet face fool you

hand goes back and forth

lots of frilly layers

what evil lurks in these pockets?

plugs in

shoes glued to the base . . . or is she ready to pounce?

And that
gives Josh
an idea . . .

We rig up Mrs. Claus to prank Mom.

Armload of clean towels ends up on the floor.

We're on the floor too— laughing.

Unfortunately, it's easy to see what's coming.
Mom's so upset she can't even spit out a
complete sentence.

You kids put more time into joking around than—

If you put this much energy into unpacking and getting ready for school—

Do you even remember that school starts in—

I don't like that doll! It's not a Santa and I don't like it!

Cheezers. She's exploding. Next she'll either ground
us or give us more work to do. We pick up the
towels and put them away and then we all run in
different directions. She can't catch all of us.

I take refuge at the library for the second time today. It's becoming my home-away-from-new-house-away-from-real-home, the one we moved out of. I tell Miss Claire about the prank. She laughs and hands me a new book she thinks I'll like.

And she introduces me to . . .

Glenda.

You're both in sixth grade at King Elementary!

I can tell you're new here. Everyone else has been here forever. It's a good place to live. My great-great-grandparents were even born here! More than a hundred years ago! One of the kids at school is my cousin, and two are my second cousins, and I think some others are my first cousins twice removed or else my second cousins once removed. But anyway . . .

She looks like a poodle.

I can't remember what else she says, because basically she says nothing, a lot.

47

When I'm talking to Glenda my brain can slither out of my body, out the window, take a walk in the garden, plant a tree and watch it grow, then yank itself back inside, sit back down in my head, start listening again, and never miss anything important! But suddenly Glenda mentions . . . games.

Every year, the last week of summer, the whole neighborhood plays big games like hide-and-seek and capture the flag. It's a blast. You have to come! We meet near school at the giant beech tree at seven.

Sounds great!

Tonight?

Tomorrow.

Glenda can't hang out because she's going school shopping. I don't even want to think about that. I need some friends. On the way back to the house, I notice these clues.

Clue	Deduction	Yeah, but . . .
	Someone older than 4 owns it.	Could be some old guy.
	Probably not an old guy.	Oh, joy. A friend for the monkey boy.
	Also probably not an old guy.	Some toddler is pretty rough on her doll!
	A tree house! I love tree houses. This could be a friendship worth pursuing.	The railing is broken. The kid is probably in the hospital after falling out of it.
	Woods. Something potentially very cool.	It's late. I'll check it out tomorrow.

I wake up from a dream about my old friends hating me for moving away and finding new friends. It feels so real, and so painful. My throat feels thick. My stomach feels like someone sat on it all night. I miss them. Do they miss me? I have to get out of here. What's in those woods?

Answer:

A well-hidden nest

A woodpecker

Deer tracks—but no deer

Lots of burrs (nature's Velcro)

Spiderwebs strung across the path

Aside from the spiderwebs, I love this. I claim these woods for ME. They're mine!

I am Sacajawea, exploring a new land. This could be my own secret hideout. If I ever have to get away from everyone I can come here. But soon I discover that someone else has been here.

I use the trash to dig a hole for the trash and then bury it. These don't really feel like my woods anymore.

Looking up, the trees and sky look like jigsaw puzzle pieces that don't quite fit.

Funny, that's how I feel: like I don't quite fit. I like the library and Miss Claire. Glenda's okay. These woods are okay. But I dread school. I miss my friends. I don't want to make new friends. It's a hassle.

Walking along, I come to the perfect place for lunch.

A river, a bent tree bridge, a little waterfall, a turtle, zillions of pretty rocks, some fossils. It's perfect, except—

53

Oh, great. A boy.

#1 I don't like being called the new kid, even if it's true.

#2 I don't like being spied on. How else would he know I'm new here?

#3 It's not the Sweeneys' house anymore. I don't feel like it's ours really, but it's definitely not the Sweeneys'.

He offers me half a granola bar and I'm hungry so I take it. We talk.

Travis

He lives around the block from me. Like everyone else, he was born here. He has three sisters. He likes English stuff (he went to London a few weeks ago) and cartooning (hey—so do I!).

I tell him I miss my old house and my old friends because they were the best. But I'll probably never see them again and they'll forget me. My throat hurts again so I quit talking. I kind of expect him to say I'll get new friends or this is a better place than where I used to live—but he doesn't.

He just says, "Life goes on, whether we want it to or not." And that's pretty much it. The world keeps turning no matter how miserable I get.

I'm hungry, I don't want to leave, and I have lunch in my backpack. So I share it. He tells me about London.

"Mind the gap." It's on T-shirts and signs, hats, mugs, mouse pads, everything. It means "watch your step between the subway and the platform."

They also have living statues—people painted all in gray, even their hair, and they stand really still. It's street theater!

They have different words for normal boring things that make them sound more interesting. Like *queue* (pronounced like the letter *Q*). It just means long lines people stand in.

I wish my family had moved to London instead of here.

After a while, we start to head back.

On the way, he shows me the weirdest plant I've ever seen— the Touch-Me-Not. It's pretty, with yellowish orange and reddish brown speckles.

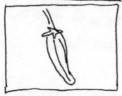

When you touch the seedpod,

it unpeels like a spring-loaded banana and shoots out a seed!

And each tendril curls up. It's so funny. We do it again and again: touch the seedpod, watch it spring, laugh hysterically.

target shooting

Sproing!

I take this as a challenge. Now I have to find something cool to show Travis. At the edge of the woods, I notice a walking stick on a log. I've seen these at camp a few times.

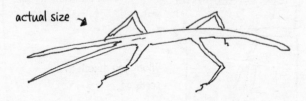

actual size ➤

They look like little tree branches that walk (ver-r-ry slowly). I pick him up gently and put him on Travis's arm.

Nice find.

But it's too good to last. We say good-bye.

Back at my house, I'm reminded of the realities of life . . .

Huge mess in progress, which I get stuck cleaning up.

I tell Mom and Dad about tonight's big hide-and-seek game, but Mom doesn't want me to go out because it's getting dark (Um, Mom? Playing in the dark is the whole point!) and school starts tomorrow. She thinks I need extra time to sleep or something. Grrr. Luckily, Dad and Josh suggest a compromise to salvage my plans:

#1 Set out all my school stuff first (okay).

#2 Josh goes with me.

#3 I promise to run a lot and exhaust myself so it's easy to sleep tonight.

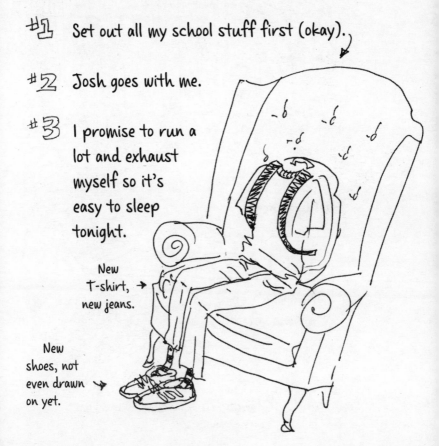

New T-shirt, → new jeans.

New shoes, not even drawn → on yet.

Josh's two new buddies, Izzy and Doof, walk with us. Why do boys have such an easy time making friends? Is there some universal boy language that makes it happen?

Ellie! Over here!

Ellie's a new kid. She doesn't know anyone yet.

Gee thanks, Glenda.

There are a lot of kids here.

Everyone makes fast introductions but I don't remember most of the names. Izzy is "it" for hide-and-seek.

To play:

One person covers his eyes and counts to 30 while everyone hides. He tries to find them. The last one he catches is the next "it." If you reach the tree before he catches you, you're safe.

Basically, I'm just running back and forth between some uninspired hiding spot and the tree.

Nobody bothers seeking or chasing me. I consider running slowly so "it" can catch me. Then I'd have to be "it," but at least people would notice I'm here. I'm at a disadvantage though. I don't know the area, or the good places to find people, so I'd probably be "it" all night.

Eventually we leave.

I've had more fun at a funeral.
Back in my room, I take inventory.

My friends:

- ☑ Miss Claire
- ☑ Ophelia (do rats count?)
- ☑ Glenda
- ☑ Travis
- ☐ Um . . .
- ☐
- ☐

11 p.m.

Ellie! Lights out! You have to get up early for school.

Okay.

2 a.m.

I'll probably fall asleep in class.

Might as well
use this time . . .

What I Want
from School:

- Fast, easy friendships.
- Nice, smart teachers who are also funny.
  Bonus: good looking.
- No embarrassing events.
- Tasty lunches.
- No school dances.
- Lots of sports and academic games.
- No films, lectures, or tests that make me
  fall asleep. (Ha! I could use one of those
  right now!)
- No cheesy girl stuff: no dressing up fancy,
  no boy-girl stuff, no overexposure to pink.
  Just normal stuff: books, cool experiments,
  art, music, field trips.

I think that covers every possible problem. If I
expect good things, then good things will come,
right? Good night.

The big day.
Dad gives us a pep talk over breakfast.

Josh puts my lunch money in an upside-down glass of water. Trying to get it out, I soak my shirt and have to change. Grrr.

Mom always takes a First Day of School photo:

We all wish we were back home at our old schools.

Mom and Dad bribed Risa with voice lessons (the top music teacher in the state teaches at Risa's new high school). So Risa's okay being here.

Josh can keep up with his old friends online, plus he already made friends with Izzy and Doof, so he's okay.

Me? I have NOTHING.

The Torture Chamber:

#1 Deep breaths.

#2 Expect good things.

#3 Take one little step at a time.

One of those groups is the right group for me.

The bell rings.

The doors open and everyone starts banging into each other, bumping into walls, trying to form a very disorganized line. We file past the teachers at the door and then there's no line anymore. Just chaos. All I know is I'm supposed to be in Room 23 upstairs. I sort of aim for the stairwell and I become part of a zillion-legged caterpillar, moving up the stairs without even thinking. Don't fall, don't fall, don't fall. That's all I have in my brain.

And it's really, really loud.

Above the crowd, I see a window, high on the wall, straight ahead. I aim for it. The crowd turns to go down the hallway but I stand at the window wall for a minute, checking that my things survived the surge:

My backpack is still on my back.
My shoes are still on my feet.
My head is still attached to my neck.
I guess I'm okay.

I take a deep breath and plunge back into the caterpillar crowd, letting it walk me around corner after corner until finally I see Room 23— and Glenda!

You goof! What'd you come that way for? Everyone knows you take the back door. It's a lot less crowded.

Sure. Everyone except ME.

Rather than freak out on Glenda, I calmly hang my backpack on one of the little baby coat hooks in the hallway (any respectable school would have lockers).

She goes off to her class, next door. I stand there looking stupid. All the girls are wearing dresses!

Thank goodness the bell rings.

I take a seat in the back so I can see everything. The teacher makes everyone move forward to fill the empty seats but my row is full. So now I'm the only person at the back of the room.

Mrs. Whittam calls each student's name. She calls me Eleanor McDuggle. I try to correct her but she must not hear me because she says, "Okay, Ella."

Mrs. Whittam explains the Important Procedures we'll do every morning:

- Find our name in the can, ⟵ Ugh!

- Check the board for homework,
- Sharpen pencils before the bell rings, and
- Say the Pledge of Allegiance and the School Pledge.

I pledge to myself, on this day, to try to be kind, in . . .

I don't know the words.

I feel like an idiot.

And now everyone thinks my name is Ella. Argghh!

> I hate this school.
> I hate this school.
> I hate this school.

Sitting in the back is a disadvantage. I can't see anyone's face. Don't know the names. This is what they look like to me.

Eventually it's lunchtime.

Ding!

But we're still in line for food when the five-minute warning bell rings. So we get a whopping ten seconds to eat AND get outside for recess before we have to get back to class.

This happens every year.

As for the food (if you can call it that):

Ryan testing the rubberiness quotient of the hot dogs.

Recess:

Yeah. Right.
No thank you.

Then on to Mr.
Brendall's class for
the afternoon.

Reading, writing,
history, and civics
in the morning with
Mrs. Whittam.
Science, math, and
geography in the
afternoon with
Mr. Brendall.

In Mr. Brendall's class, I sit in the front row. But it has the same effect: I can't see anyone! Cheezers! But then, a miracle.

So, even though every girl is in a dress except me, and even though everyone got my name wrong except Travis and Glenda, maybe somehow this will all work out?

But then Mr. Brendall calls roll:

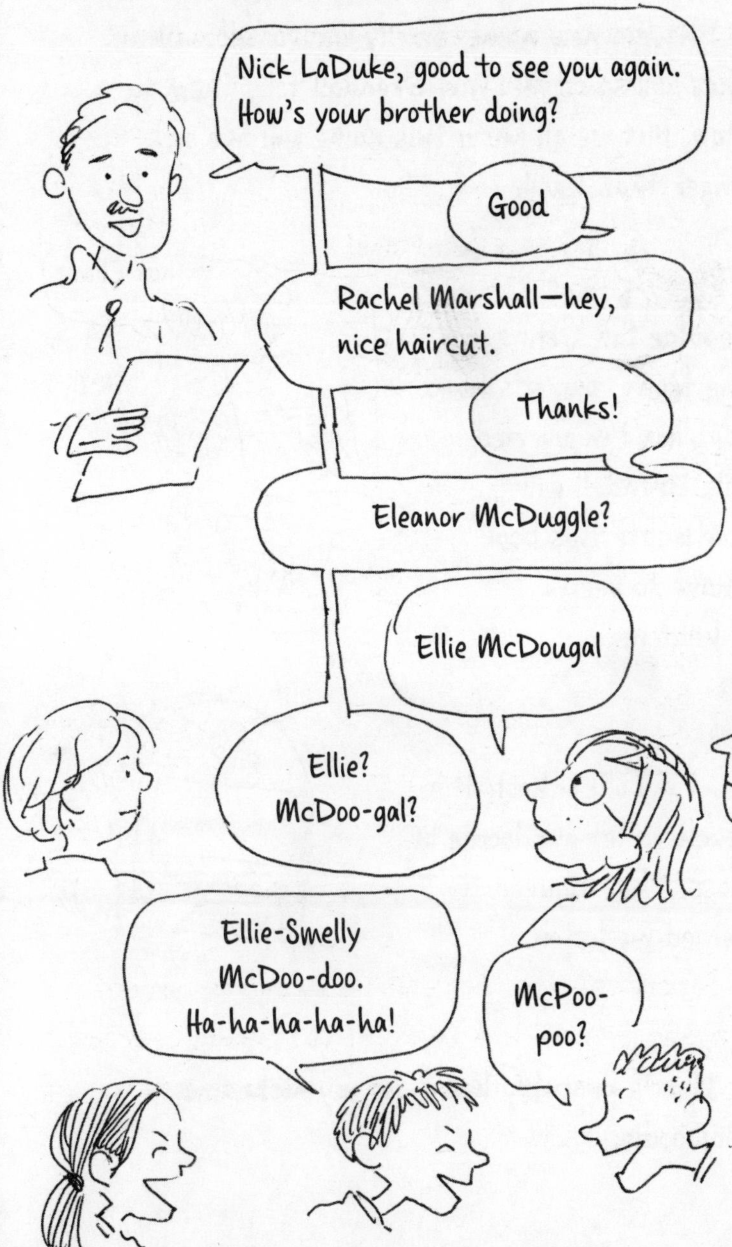

Wonderful.

I have a new name: Smelly McDoo-doo. Oh, they are so clever. Mr. Brendall tells them to stop, but we all know this name will live on longer than I will.

Since I'm sitting in the front row, it's hard to draw. I'm worried Mr. Brendall will confiscate this book. I have to keep it hidden.

At my old school, the teachers let me doodle in class. They figured it helped me listen.

R.I.P.

My name

never heard
again

That's probably how I got my nickname, McDoodle.

Mr. Brendall says we're going to play missing person since we all got to know each other in Mrs. Whittam's room.

Jake is the first detective. He goes out in the hallway.

Once he's out there, Mr. Brendall picks someone to be the missing person. He picks Zoey, who hides.

Everyone else moves to a new seat. The detective comes back and tries to guess who is missing. He gets three tries.

Then the missing person (Zoey) comes out, everyone laughs, and the detective picks a new detective to go out in the hall. The missing person picks a replacement too, and the game continues.

We play a few rounds. Mo picks me to be the detective, and I don't feel so left out. But my three guesses are all wrong because I don't recognize very many people in the class. If they all turned around and showed me the backs of their heads, THEN maybe I could identify them!

But it's a fun game, even though I'm no good at it.

At the end . . .

Hey, Ellie, I like your art.

Thanks, Travis.

It's good, but I like Rachel's better. She's our class artist.

Everyone leaves at the end of the day, and I'm not sure whether I'm glad school is over or if I wish I had more time there.

Bye, Ellie. See you tomorrow. Hey, do you want to come to my house today? We can hang out.

Huh?

Oh, how I just love it when the right words just spring from my lips, making me look sooo intelligent.

Luci?

I'll have to ask my mom. I'll call you if it's okay. What's your phone number?

Um.

It's uh . . .

I remember eventually.

Oh, great. Mrs. Claus is SUCH a warm welcome home after a long day. Especially waving a plastic knife. I guess the fake candle just wasn't scary enough for Josh.

I have to think of a way to get even.

RINGGG!

Risa answers.

Who is Luci?

She's a girl in my class. Give me the phone.

Not so fast. What does she want?

What do you mean, what does she want? She wants to talk to me! She wants me to come over!

First you have to clean the kitchen. It's your turn.

We didn't eat dinner yet! I'll clean it after dinner. I'm telling Mom.

Mom left me in charge while she's at work, and I want the breakfast dishes done before dinner.

I'll tell Luci to call you back later.

Risa says if I don't do the dishes NOW, she'll make me clean the bathroom too. Grrr. See? I'm a powerless pawn!

People move me to new houses and new schools without even caring how I feel.

People push me around in the hallways.

They make me do all the work, and if I speak up, I get punished with MORE work.

Eventually, I'm ready.

Packing for Luci's House:
I don't really know Luci. She sits behind me in Mr. Brendall's class, and we said a few words when I handed back papers. So what do I bring to her house? I decide to bring everything:

☐ two library books
☐ paper, colored pencils, markers
☐ hiking stuff: water bottle, bandana, animal tracks book
☐ CDs of my favorite music
☐ this book

Off to Luci's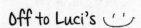

90

Got it.

Great!

Beep Boop
Beep Boop
Beep !

I'll get my turn pretty soon . . .

Beep
Beep
Boop

Beep   Beep   Boop
Boop   Beep   Beep
Beep   Beep

This is the most incredibly boring time I ever had in my whole life.

Beep
Beep
Boop

Well, I have to go now.

Okay, see you in school tomorrow.

Boop
Beep

Come over again tomorrow. This was fun.

Maybe . . .

I run all the way home and find . . .

My socks, all knotted together!

Somebody (my guess is Josh) has tied all of my socks together in one long string and hung them all over the front of our house. Aargh!

93

This is so typical. Josh has been playing tricks on me since I was a toddler:

I'm torn between wanting revenge and wanting to stay on his good side.

Dinner. I choose revenge. Amazingly, the whole family plays along.

Please pass the potatoes.

Potatoes? You want some?

Yes . . .

Okay, but Risa wants some first.

Sure. Thanks, Ellie. Mom, while they're here, want some?

Why yes, thanks. Maybe Dad does too.

Thanks, yes, but I feel bad for Josh, who's waiting, so let's pass these back to Mom.

Risa, pass these to Josh.

But they'll get to Josh faster going the other way.

Right. I'll pass them to Dad.

You know, I really think they'll get to Josh faster if they go to Ellie . . .

Josh doesn't hold a grudge. He thinks all pranks are funny, even the ones we play on him. He helps me do the dishes and he says it's so we can get to the neighborhood game faster. But I think it's so I will owe him.

Ellie, if I am not dismayed, what am I? Mayed?

Uh

Oxygen is not an inert gas. So does that make it ert?

Tie, untie. Common, uncommon. Do, undo. If "I understand" means I get it, does "I derstand" mean the opposite?

How to Play Ghost in the Graveyard

Pick someone to be ghost. Everyone else is a victim.

Victims stand at gool (the safe spot). In our case, gool is the big tree.

The ghost hides while the victims cover their eyes and slowly count the hours till midnight:

> 1:00, 2:00, 3:00, 4:00, 5:00, 6:00, 7:00, 8:00, 9:00, 10:00, 11:00, MIDNIGHT! Hope I don't see a ghost tonight!

The victims search for the ghost. When a victim finds the ghost, they run away yelling:

> GHOST IN THE GRAVEYARD!

The ghost chases all the victims back to gool. If the ghost catches a victim, the victim becomes the new ghost.

Travis and I figure out a way to work together to never get caught. We position ourselves so each can see half of the yard.

Travis watches this side.

I watch this side.

When we see the ghost coming, we signal so we both have a chance to escape. It's very effective.

Run!

But pretty soon the others figure out what we're doing and they target us.

This is way too much fun. I'm screaming and laughing my head off.
Good news: I'm meeting more kids.
Bad news: they aren't in my class at school, except Travis.

Arleen

gool

99

Travis tells the funniest joke right when I am drinking some water and I spit it all over myself. (And some on him too. Sorry, Travis, it's your own fault!)

I tell my best joke and Arleen tells hers and pretty soon we're laughing at anything.

Maybe a joke is funnier when:
1) you like the person who tells it, and
2) you're already laughing.

Bummer. It's time to go home. I knew this was too good to last.

Trying to remember all of Travis's and Arleen's jokes:

-Knock, knock!
-Who's there?
-Amish.
-Amish who?
-You don't look like a shoe!

-Knock, knock!
-Who's there?
-Cows go.
-Cows go who?
-No, silly, cows go MOO!

-Knock, knock!
-Who's there?
-Little old lady.
-Little old lady who?
-I didn't know you could yodel!

-What do you get from a pampered cow?
-Spoiled milk.

-What did the cannibals do at the wedding?
-They toasted the bride and groom.

-Knock, knock!
-Who's there?
-Interrupting cow.
-Interrupting c—
-MOO!

-Knock, knock!
-Who's there?
-What.
-What who?
-Sorry, only one question at a time.

-What has five eyes and a mouth?
-The Mississippi River.

-What do you get when you cross beans with an onion?
-Tear gas.

-Knock, knock!
-Who's there?
-Woo.
-Woo who?
-Don't get so excited, it's just a joke.

-Knock, knock!
-Who's there?
-Noah.
-Noah who?
-Noah good place to find more jokes?

-Why did the streetlight turn red?
-It was caught changing in the street.

On the second day of school I wear a dress.
Everyone else is in PANTS. I can't win.

Mrs. Whittam still calls me Ella.
And I'm having trouble learning who is who.
It's not my fault. Everyone has too many names,
especially the boys!

Oochie:
the teachers
call him Dave

Louise:
also known
as Wheezer

Ed Sparrow:
aka Bird
or Beaker

In class we discuss nonviolent protests, since the school is named for Martin Luther King Jr. I should nonviolently protest how they keep messing up my name. And our move to this city. And dresses.

One good thing: we get to move our desks into groups: I'm with Mo, Travis, and the kid who bounces hot dogs. And another: in two days we start safety patrol. That's something we could volunteer for at my old school. You know, the school where nobody wore dresses.

Art class should be fun, right? It's not.

The teacher is just plain strange.

She's also very pointy.

She says we can't use black paint in our art, ever.

I think she's a lousy artist.

And her breath stinks.

Ms. Trebuchet* gives our first assignment: find a texture in the room and draw it up close. Most of the kids draw the tiles on the floor or ceiling or the heating vents or the venetian blinds. I use artistic license and draw Ophelia's tail.

*pronounced Treh-bu-shay

I love my drawing. I ♡ Ophelia.

Who drew this WORM? Is this a joke?

I try to defend my art. I'm thinking she never saw a real rat before. Maybe I should bring Ophelia in to prove my art is good.

Eleanor, if you want to become a real artist you'd better follow my rules.

Speaking of rules, I remember that I didn't follow the morning procedure in Mrs. Whittam's class so now I might not have any lunch. I ask to go to the principal's office to reserve a lunch.

Walking out the door, I think of a new symbol:
∧ means the opposite of love.
I ∧ art class. I ∧ Ms. Trebuchet.
  In the hallway, I find this.

My
stomach hurts.
I ∧ this school.
I ∧ everyone here.

Lunchtime. Mo grabs my elbow and pushes me in front of her in line. I try to smile, but I'm really trying not to burst out crying. I show her the bingo note.

I wipe away a tear and some kid yells, "Bingo!"

There's really nothing anyone can say to make me feel better. They can't defend this. There's too much wrong with this place. I want to go home—my real home, not this awful new home.

At recess I just want to be alone but Mo and Travis won't let me. It's kind of annoying. They should go join everyone else and play soccer, but they keep hanging around me.

In the afternoon, I try not to do anything I saw on the bingo note. During math, Mo makes me a fortune-teller cootie catcher:

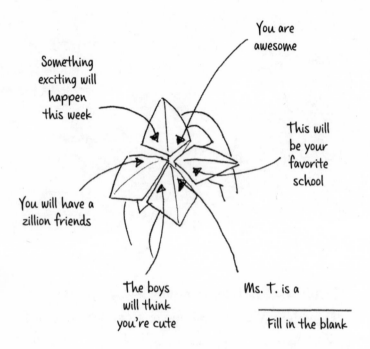

You are awesome

Something exciting will happen this week

This will be your favorite school

You will have a zillion friends

The boys will think you're cute

Ms. T. is a
_____
Fill in the blank

It's goofy, but it's nice of Mo to make it. So I make her a piano. Origami counts as a math exercise, right? Sort of?

How to Make a
Fortune-Teller Cootie Catcher

(skip to ④ if you have
a square sheet of paper)

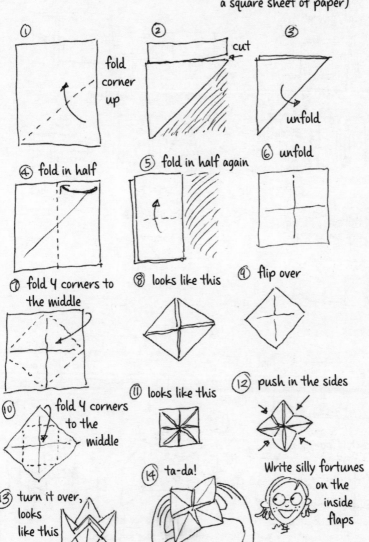

① fold corner up

② cut

③ unfold

④ fold in half

⑤ fold in half again

⑥ unfold

⑦ fold 4 corners to the middle

⑧ looks like this

⑨ flip over

⑩ fold 4 corners to the middle

⑪ looks like this

⑫ push in the sides

⑬ turn it over, looks like this

⑭ ta-da!

Write silly fortunes on the inside flaps

How to Make an Origami Piano

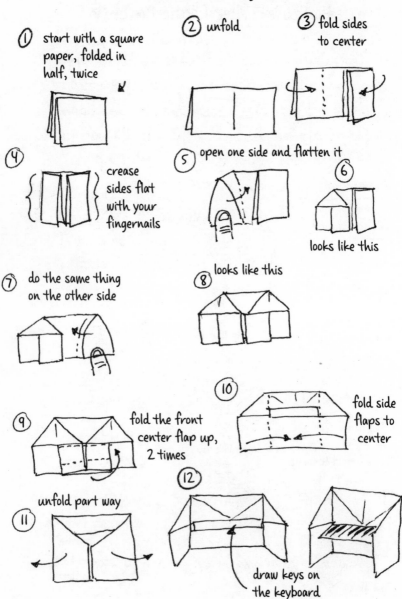

① start with a square paper, folded in half, twice

② unfold

③ fold sides to center

④ crease sides flat with your fingernails

⑤ open one side and flatten it

⑥ looks like this

⑦ do the same thing on the other side

⑧ looks like this

⑨ fold the front center flap up, 2 times

⑩ fold side flaps to center

⑪ unfold part way

⑫ draw keys on the keyboard

Walking home from school, I have mixed feelings. Some parts of this place I like. Some parts I 💗 a lot.

I wonder what my old friends are doing now. Do they miss me? I should work on the group journal tonight. I keep forgetting it. But I don't want to put all this bad stuff in it. I'll wait until something good happens.

I decide to stop in at the library and see Miss Claire. Oh, this is terrible . . .

Well hello, Ellie! I want you to meet a dear friend of mine, Lavonne Trebuchet. She's an artist too.

I mumble hi and make an excuse to leave, fast.

At home, I pop into the kitchen for a snack . . .

this book ↗

Ahem. Looks like Dad had a run-in with Mrs. Claus.
I know better than to stick around!

Cheezers!
Josh was here.
Even the posters
are upside down.

It's
a relief when
Mo calls to
invite me
to her house
for dinner.

Mo's family seems so gentle and nice.

I already know Mo has a big heart!

Her dad works at the corner gas station and brings home a lot of expiring-today snacks. Mo gives me a big bag of chips to bring home for my family—they taste okay to me. Josh will probably eat the whole bag today. Mo's sister, Diana, is 5 and adorable. Thomas is 14 and has Down syndrome. Mo's mom seems very unstressed—unlike my mom!

Moonie, the dog, is big and scary looking but Mo says he's a teddy bear.

I feel very comfortable. Mo and I are hanging out, listening to music. Thomas wants to hang out too, and that's okay until . . .

I don't want to. I really, really don't want to. But how do I say no?

I've read hundreds of books and none of them ever told me what to do in this sort of situation.

At dinner, Thomas sits so close to me he's practically on my chair. Mo acts like this is completely normal. I try not to seem too weirded out. New revelation: I'm a personal-space kind of girl!

So, Ellie. Mo tells us you're an artist. What kind of art do you like to do most?

Uh, simple cartoony stuff. Nothing too complicated or crowded.

I've never seen Thomas react like this.

Ha-ha! Maybe he's in love.

I get a big hug good-bye from Thomas and Diana.

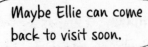
Maybe Ellie can come back to visit soon.

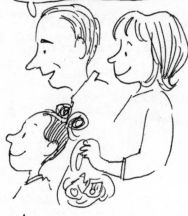

Mo walks me halfway home.

Ellie, thanks for being so nice to Thomas. Most people are awkward around him. In fact, I hardly ever have friends over because of it.

You're a hero.

Whoa. Mo seems like a girl who has everything she wants. I never guessed pieces of her life don't always fit. She's more like me than I thought—another jigsaw puzzle with too many pieces!

When I get to my block, the neighborhood kids are playing capture the flag. I stash my bag of chips in a bush and join the game in progress, basically helping Travis's team lose. Sorry about that!

<-- Ambush in waiting. -->

Hurry! Quick!

How to Play Capture the Flag

Each team hides its flag (decide on rules like how far off the ground, how visible it should be, etc.). Then everyone gets a job:

Some kids guard. The sneakers go into enemy territory to search for the other flag. The rangers catch prisoners and throw them in jail. You can get thrown in jail just for being on the other team's property. But they have to catch you first! And the rangers also try to get their own team out of the enemy jail without getting caught. First team to capture the other team's flag wins!

Too soon it's time to go inside.

Josh razzes me about losing. I push him, and pretty soon we're play-fighting.

Attack of the twins!

The twins are his STINKY feet.

I dive for my secret weapon: Josh's water bottle.

But to my utter shock . . .

. . . Josh has been training Ben-Ben to be HIS secret weapon!

Empty!

Very full!

They out-strategize me completely. This is a lot of fun, but I don't know if I will ever get even with Josh. He always wins.

Good night.

This is the scene at breakfast the next day:

Oh yeah? Well, you're a LERT.

You're a DEPT.

You're a NONYMOUS.

And YOU are a NOTHER!

You're a BNORMAL!

You're a RITHMETIC!

um . . .

You're a FFLICTED!

uh . . .

I win!

Meanwhile, Ben-Ben's stuffing his nose with cereal. He even figures out a way to hang the cereal from his nostrils. My family is so talented.

Amid the madness, Ophelia and I try to share a bowl of cereal.

She's the perfect antidote to crazy people. Which gives me a very good idea.

You brought a RAT to demonstrate nonviolent protest?

Well, yes. That, and also for art class, to show textures.

Hmm. Okay. Explain the protest part.

I think fast . . .

She says:
Ellie, you could have just brought a flute.

True, but I notice this: Mrs. Whittam calls me by the right name. Finally!

Well, the Pied Piper of Hamelin led all of the rats out of town, but then the people refused to pay him so he protested by leading the children away too, using nothing but a flute.

Unfortunately, not everyone does. I've been called:

Allie
Ella
Eleanor
Elmo
Smellie
Ollie

Cheezers. My name isn't THAT hard to learn.
Here's something cool I discover on my calculator
during spelling:

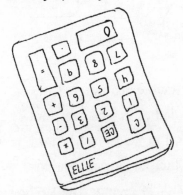

31773 = ELLIE
0.7734 = hELLO
14 = W
7735 = SELL
7738 = BELL
379919 = GIGGLE

Mrs. Whittam tells me to put away my calculator
until math class. And this sketchbook too.

At least Ophelia's having fun. She's rolling
around the room in her rodent ball, bumping into
chairs, making some of the girls scream, which
makes me 379919.

We're in a long, unmoving lunch line yet AGAIN. We're the last class to get lunch—that's why it takes so long. Mo and I sit down and pretty soon the whole class is sitting. It's a sit-in!

Me   Mo   Nikki   Cody   Travis

But apparently we're having too much fun, because one of the lunch ladies comes over and makes us stand up. Grrr. I'm mad now! I start writing a letter to the principal (a polite letter). Nikki says it's no use trying to change the system because it's always been like this. But I say if you aren't willing to work to change something, then you deserve what you have.

Nikki asks if Mo and I want to come to her house after school. Mo's busy (piano lessons) but I say yes!

In Mr. Brendall's class I get to demonstrate some of Ophelia's tricks.

I tell the class that rats are like puppies. You can teach them to do just about anything for a treat.

This trick makes everyone say "ewww!" Nikki says when I come over tonight to leave my rat at home.

Ms. Trebuchet doesn't like rats.

Ms. Trebuchet doesn't want to hear about whether Ophelia's tail looks like the drawing I did yesterday.

Out, NOW.

Mrs. Trebuchet is a

> Pointy
> Artist
> In
> Noir.

Noir = French for "black."

When I take Ophelia back to Mr. Brendall's classroom, Cody takes my seat in art class, which means I have to sit in the front row. Bleah.

How can Ms. Trebuchet be friends with Miss Claire anyhow? It just doesn't fit.

Ms. T shows us pictures of Georgia O'Keefe's flower art. I like learning about other artists.

Georgia O'Keefe took photos of flowers close up. So now we're supposed to draw flowers close up. Do we get real flowers to draw from? No. Plastic flowers to use as models? No.

Ms. T wants us to copy other artists' drawings of flowers. How is this art? Making Ms. T mad won't help anything, so I don't complain. But I can't resist asking, "What's the point?" Mo snickers. I try hard not to giggle myself.

Ms. T gives a straight answer: the masters learned by copying other artists.

Oh.

I'm not the only one who brought something to art class today.

Rachel, the "school artist," spent all summer making a puppet that spits out smoke. I admit, it's cool. It's for some big contest that Ms. T told the class about last June. I guess I don't get to enter since I didn't know anything about it. I △ being the new kid! I bet I'll wear this label until high school.

N for New Kid

But then after class, Ms. T pulls me aside.

Miss Claire and Miss Whittam both told me about your art, and I've been peeking at your book in class. Your work is good! I think you should enter the same contest as Rachel.

Me, in total shock.

I bought you a pad of bristol paper to use for it. Maybe you could do one of your cartoons? There isn't much time, I'm afraid. It's due Friday. Do you want to try?

Yes!

And thanks!

I'm not sure what to draw. It has to be great to win. This will be tough.

At home, I inspect my new art paper.

This is very fancy
and expensive drawing
paper. It's so smooth. So beautiful. Ms. Trebuchet
said, "It takes an ink line nicely." There are 50
sheets, which means I can make a mistake 49
times. I'm almost afraid of it! Especially since I

have no idea
what to draw.
I'm going
to Nikki's
instead!

The inside of Nikki's house looks like a palace. It's hard to believe people live as nicely as this.

They sit on thrones to eat dinner!

My family would not do well with such wealth.

#1 How would we play "Don't Pass the Potatoes to Josh" at such a huge table?

#2 Risa would act even MORE like a princess.

Nikki and I hang out in her giant playroom.

Wall-sized dollhouse.

That's a TV.

Secret passage to Nikki's room.

Sound system that would make a radio station jealous. I could sit here all day and read her graphic novel collection.

But Nikki gets bored and wants to go to the mall.

So Nikki's nanny packs up her little brother, Wellington, and drives us to the mall. The nanny gives us an hour to shop.

Oooh! Look at that.

I have to have that!

New shirt from Nikki.

Nikki's bags.

If I ever win a shopping spree, I'm calling Nikki to help me spend it. She's talented at this.

Back at my small, cluttered, but never boring
house, it's dinnertime.

Hey, Ellie, I fork-ot to grab a fork.
Get me one?

Here.

Thanks.

Then Josh sticks
the fork up his nose
and digs out a ton of
green goop.

Josh.

Turns out it was guacamole
in his hand, not his nose.

Ben-Ben thinks it's
hilarious.

HOW DISGUSTING!

After dinner, I try to figure out what to draw for the art contest. Make a mini-sketchbook? Think of a new board game? There's not enough time for something so elaborate.

Posters still upside down— thanks to Josh

I've never felt so paralyzed and so uncreative.

Staring at the blank page only makes me feel worse. I can't tell Ms. Trebuchet. She's counting on me to do something "wonnnderful."

I rack my brain for two hours, then climb into bed. I have to get to school early tomorrow for safety patrol.

Rules for Safety Patrol:
1) Wear the plastic fluorescent orange vest.
2) Pay attention when you're on post.
3) Keep kids safe from traffic.
4) Don't let anyone in the school early.

    I get stuck at the kindergarten doors with Glenda.
1) These vests glow in the dark. Sooo fashionable.
2) Does paying attention mean I have to listen to
    Glenda? She talks A LOT.
3) This is a useless job. There's no traffic here. I
    doubt there will be a mad rush to get in school
    early. More like a mad rush to get OUT early.

Goofy vests, eh?

Yes! This orange doesn't match anything. And it doesn't rhyme with anything, either. Blah, blah . . .

We're just getting settled into Mrs. Whittam's class when the principal, Mrs. Ping, comes in to talk about my letter.

Boys and girls, hello. I'd like to take this opportunity to thank Ella for bringing this situation to my attention. I agree, it's serious. Blah, blah, blah, so we have a solution, Ella, and now I consider this matter to be resolved. Thank you.

Ellie!

Ellie!

Mrs. Ping says a whole lot of nothing when she talks. Still, if this means getting to eat lunch on time, maybe it will be worth the embarrassment?

Mrs. Ping's Solution:

Our class goes first at lunchtime. Our class is happy. The problem is solved.

Well, it's about time.

That was so unfair.

That was so smart of Ellie to write a letter!

But the OTHER sixth grade class is mad because now THEY'RE at the end of the line.

Why do WE have to go last?

Why did they change this?

I heard it's that new girl Ella's fault.

I'd be happy just getting my lunch and eating it, but no. I'm involved to the bitter end. Cheezers.

Ellie, you have to do something.

I DID! It didn't do any good.

Well, you have to do something more.

We'll help you!

Okay. Plan B. Tell Mrs. Ping that switching the order of the sixth grade classes is not an acceptable solution.

Dear Mrs. Ping,

After today's lunch, it's clear the solution of switching who goes first at lunch doesn't solve the problem. When my class went last, people weren't mad at me. Now they are. What if we switch back so my class goes last, but we speed up the line instead?

Sincerely,
Ellie McDougal

There. That should settle it.

In the afternoon we play one round of Mr. Brendall's patented Quick Computations. He rattles off a bunch of equations in a row and we keep a running tally. Anyone who gets the right answer at the end gets a free lunch in the cafeteria.

For me, there's no such thing as free lunch. I'm not brokenhearted.

After school at Mo's we're goofing around, adding new lyrics to old music, when Thomas comes in.

Before heading home I draw Thomas
and Diana as cartoon paper dolls
they can cut out.

Then I run all the way home because suddenly
I HAVE AN IDEA FOR MY ART PROJECT!

Risa is sometimes uncooperative. Luckily, this isn't one of those times. Plus, she respects art so she's willing to drive me to the art store . . .

And she gets a clerk to help us load our stuff in the car, and I sketch my idea while she spends a half hour flirting with the clerk. (Peter, age 18, likes to paint and has some art in a gallery in town. The opening is tomorrow night and now we're invited.)

Then I lock myself in my room and start creating.

I turn in my finished project first thing in the morning.

Lightweight foam board.

It's me!

Foam board sketch pad has sketches of my new house, the woods, friends, family, and school— all inspired from THIS book. My foam board T-shirt says, "Artists draw on the world for inspiration . . . and to inspire."

Then I join Glenda at the kindergarten door.
I'm so happy my project is done, I don't even
mind her chatter.

In Mrs. Whittam's class we start creative
writing. Our first assignment is to write a letter
to a newspaper editor about a historical issue
that concerns us, like grape boycotts and
segregation laws. She says it's a form of
nonviolent protest. We don't really send them,
but we address the envelopes anyhow.

And Mrs.
Whittam
winks at me.

Lunchtime:

Mrs. Ping must have gotten my letter because my class is last in line again. I try to put a good spin on it.

We could do a line dance?

Yeah!

Get it? A long line dance?

We try doing the wave. Nothing works. I'm thinking of Mrs. Whittam's wink. We have only one option left: action. I make up a battle cry:

> Always believe: cowards don't excel. From Ghandi's harrowing intellectual journey, King-ites learned many nonviolent options. Philosophical questions rise, surely. They're unimportant! Victorious, we're xenial youthful zealots.

Okay, it's too long for a battle cry. But it will work as our nonviolent manifesto. All we have to do now is figure out what to do and do it. Xenial? Means good at hospitality; we need a better X word!

In Mr. Brendall's class, I obsess over lunch lines.

Math:

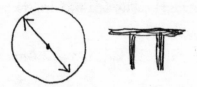

Pi: an irrational, unending number, the ratio of a circle's circumference to its diameter.

Pie: A lunch dessert rarely eaten because there's no time for it. Served in an irrationally long, unending line circling the room.

More Math:

We convert feet to inches. Question: If there are 55 kids in a lunch line and each has 2 feet, how many inches long is the line?

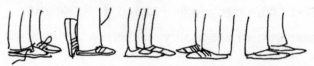

Science:

Explain observations: lunch lines are too long.

Measurement of data: 55 kids in line simultaneously.

Analysis of data: 30 kids get a very short lunch.

Graphing:

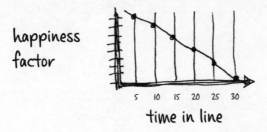

happiness factor

time in line

Prediction model: long lines for the rest of the year if we students don't do something to change it.

Test hypothesis: Monday—we have two days to plan.

Evaluate how data fit: empty stomachs versus full?

Communicate findings: already tried two letters to the principal. Next: a letter to the newspaper editor?

In the hallway, I grab Mo, Travis, and Glenda.

We have to do something. We have to come in on Monday with a big plan or I will go crazy.

Let's meet.

At the library.

At four.

Can I come too?

At home . . .

Don't forget the art gallery tonight!

No, Ben-Ben, I don't have time to push you. I have to run to the library.

We need a symbol for "no more lines." We'll plaster it EVERYWHERE—stickers, posters, T-shirts.

A symbol . . .

No more lines . . .

No queues?

No Qs?
What's that?
Like no ABCs?

No, it's British for "long line."

Oh! British, like knickers and daft and lift! We went to London—the biscuits were scrummy!

Yes, so did we!

Grrr.
Must get them back on track, brainstorming.

153

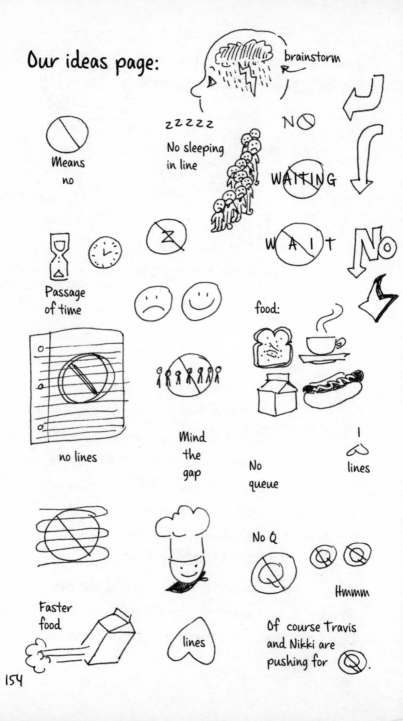

Our ideas page:

brainstorm

Means no

zzzzz
No sleeping in line

NO

WAITING

WAIT

NO

Passage of time

food:

no lines

Mind the gap

No queue

lines

Faster food

No Q

Hmmm

lines

Of course Travis and Nikki are pushing for

I say:
   Well, it's easy to read,
but we'll have to teach
the school what it means.

Travis says:
   The idea is visibility
and ease of production.

We all say:
   Huh?

Travis has the brain of an
engineer (not the train kind).
He's right. This symbol is easy to
mass produce. We'll be busy all
weekend, but we have a plan in
place, and everyone has a job.
We're all excited about this. We'll
meet back here at the library
tomorrow at 10 a.m. As for me,
I'm off to the gallery!

THE ART GALLERY

Rachel's here! We hang out because Risa is ignoring me (she's busy flirting with Peter). Also here:

Look! Free food!

Mr. Brendall!

Hello, girls.

A lady who looks like a model.

Yikes! Such weird art here.

Ms. T is here too.

There's really great stuff here too. Like Peter's:

Peter explains his philosophy of art. I don't understand most of it, but I think he's saying art should be valued and not compared because no judge is entirely fair and unbiased. Okay, but I STILL hope my Ellie foam board character wins the state art contest!

One thing I learned here tonight: there's room for all kinds of art in this world. Including my cartoons.

Cheezers. I could have predicted this.

We have so much to do in two days!
Lots to figure out:

1) How do we get the word out as widely as possible?
2) Which teachers will help us?
3) What's the best way to show off the symbol?
4) How do we make stickers?
5) Who else should we involve in the planning?
(Luci! She's great with computers. And Rachel!)

The more we do, the more I like our symbol. It's simple and easy to copy.

Things I'm learning:
The big honking dictionary at the library is an unabridged dictionary, which means it has almost every word ever known in it. We can't take it home, but we take these ones. ☞

☞ Ben-Ben's wagon.

160

I'm too busy to draw what we're doing, but we have a long list and it looks like we've covered everything. We're all painting, copying, coloring. It takes all weekend.

Tricks we figure out:

One address label sheet can hold up to 99 copies of our logo! Cut into thirds, and we have a bunch of mini stickers to hand out.

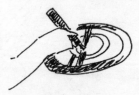

Permanent marker + cardboard stencils + a bunch of cheap T-shirts = a uniform for our group.

We break for pizza at Nikki's for lunch, and tacos for dinner, and I'm thinking I have the best group of friends in the world. Hear that? Friends.

Travis hoists our homemade flag up the pole on the school lawn.

Everyone in the group is wearing matching T-shirts.

We pose for lots of pictures.

The sidewalk is chalked.

Travis and I use our ghost in the graveyard technique to watch for teachers while Mo and Glenda hang banners.

MEANS MORE LINE

All clear on this side!

All clear here too!

We cover the hallways and
door with our
symbol.

No long = lunch lines

Less wait,
more recess

Mrs. Claus gets a position of honor by the
cafeteria door:

New Clause
in our contract—
Better food,
less wait!

Lunch lady
hairnet.

And that's when
we get caught.

Mr. Brendall and
Mrs. Whittam could
shut us down . . .

BUT THEY DON'T!!!

In fact, they help hang the sock chain and line up our foam board protesters.

Fact: the average lunch line at our school is 67 feet long. (As long as this chain of socks!)

Then Glenda and I rush to our safety posts because the kids are coming.

We have thousands
of these little stickers.

And they're being passed out
at every entrance!

And the kids love them!

Walking to class, it is so amazingly cool to see
EVERYONE wearing them.

When Mo, Travis, Rachel, Nikki, Luci, and I walk into our homeroom, the whole class stands and cheers. Mrs. Whittam doesn't stop them. It's awesome!

When the time comes to say the Pledge of Allegiance, the student voices over the public address system add a few words loud and clear, so the entire school can hear them: ". . . indivisible, with liberty and justice and SHORTER LUNCH LINES for all."

Everyone in my class bursts out laughing, and we can hear echoes of laughter from the other classrooms too.

Mrs. Whittam gives me a raised eyebrow, then starts the lesson. Which is, incidentally, a continuation of the history of nonviolent protests, and how people behave differently in a group than alone. It's the perfect lesson plan for today. I could hug her.

And then the visitors arrive . . .

Oh my gosh! It's Channel 10! That's TV. They're putting our story on TV?

By lunchtime we're all used to seeing TV cameras in the school. Mrs. Ping tries to get "our distinguished guests" to go to the front of the line, but they refuse, saying they want to eat with the students who are at the end of the line. Then they notice our huge books, which Glenda passed out as our class came in to lunch.

Why are all those kids reading in the lunch line?

Look how big the books are!

This is good. I have to get this on camera.

The line is very long and slow, so we have a whole lot of time to read . . . . or to talk about the problem with the long lines at lunch.

A half hour later we get our lunch . . .

This tastes horrid. How can you eat it?

The hot dogs set a record for bouncing!

Long lines, crummy food, hmm.

The chicken nuggets are so hard they broke my fork.

And the meatloaf is petrified! We could use it for fossil digs.

We're at the top of our game. We say everything right.

This group of creative young sixth graders at King Elementary took protest to a whole new level today . . .

We'd like to thank them for bringing this situation to our attention.

They get footage of the signs, the flag, all of it!

And we're all interviewed on live TV! Dad sees it on the news at work and rushes to our school. So do a lot of other parents.

Sport! That's a walk-off home run!

I think the whole city is here.

They give our names on the air—Ellie McDougal, Travis Owen, Mo Reilly . . . we're famous!

Even Mrs. Ping is wearing a 🚫 sticker.

And that's it. No more long lunch lines, and maybe no more bouncy hot dogs or petrified meatloaf. The TV cameras are long gone, and Dad hauled all our foam board characters and banners home for us. It seems weird to just go home, though. We decide to hold a victory celebration! Library? Can't have snacks. Somebody's house? Luci says that nobody has been to MY house yet, so that's what they all want to do. Gulp.

I warn them that at my house, anything can happen.

They see a good example of what I mean sitting on our front porch. Josh was here. Sigh. I'm nervous to go inside.

Even Miss Claire stops by. That's when I realize I'm celebrating more than just the lunchtime success at school. I'm celebrating what I've lost and found. Lost: all the sadness and worries of the past few weeks. Found: friendship. Just before everyone leaves, Ben-Ben pulls out one last surprise.

We all scream!

After the party, I finally get to work on the group journal. I have a lot to add to it before sending it back to my old friends.

Things I like about this place.

To be continued . . .

Things I've learned:

1) When I'm most sad, I should watch, because things are bound to get better.
2) A brand-new situation is like a blank canvas: I can be a real artist and make it great.
3) It's okay if new people don't like me right away. They will eventually!
4) From now on, I'm going to find the "new kid" and be friendly.

I need a new sketchbook!
This isn't the end . . . it's only the beginning.

New Kid Tips

Whether she's the new kid, or just in a new situation, here are some ideas Ellie uses to feel better.

Wear something comfortable that you love. If you're wearing your best shirt, you might feel more confident.

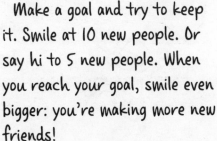

Bring something special that reminds you of good times: your favorite pencil, a heart-shaped Ellie rock (she finds those everywhere), or a lucky penny.

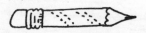

Make a goal and try to keep it. Smile at 10 new people. Or say hi to 5 new people. When you reach your goal, smile even bigger: you're making more new friends!

Are you nervous? That's normal. Just take a deep breath and trust things will work out.

Super nervous? Try yoga breathing: breathe in for 4 seconds, hold it for 4 seconds, breathe out for 4 seconds, wait for 4 seconds, and start over.

Be adventurous. Don't expect the macaroni and cheese at lunch to be the same as what's served at home. (Did you know if you hold your nose, you won't smell the food, and it won't taste quite as bad?)

Take a tip from Ben-Ben: expect to have fun, and you probably will!

New Pet? No problem.
Pet-sitting? Uh-oh . . .

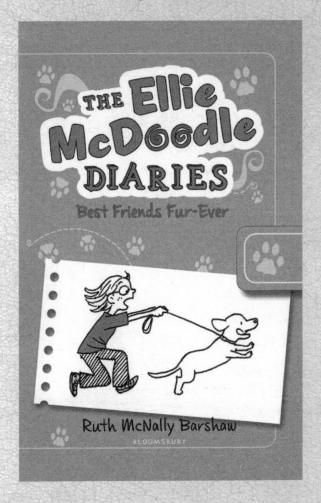

Read on for a sneak peek at
Ellie's next doodle diary

I try to catch Ben-Ben first. I didn't mean to scare him.

No! Wait! Don't cry!

Alix is circling overhead, screeching.

I'm sorry. Don't cry. It's okay. See, you're fine.

I carry Ben-Ben home while keeping an eye on Alix the whole time (and hoping I don't trip and fall). I shove Ben-Ben into the house (gently but fast!), telling him to play with the new puppy. Then I chase after Alix.

Alix is on Mrs. Morrow's roof. I try every
phrase he likes. I get his favorite treats. I extend
a broom up toward him so he can climb on it and I
can lower him back down to me. He looks at me
and walks to the back side of the roof.

I run to the backyard and call him. I beg him
to come down. Nothing works. And then . . . he
flies off!

Introducing . . .

McDoodle Words!

Ellie likes to doodle, even in her words.
In book 3, *Best Friends Fur-Ever*, Ellie starts
with a word and makes it into a McDoodle Word.
Here's how she does it.

> Step 1: Write a word on your paper.
> Example: parrot
> Step 2: Take out a letter and replace it
> with an image that explains the word.

Parrot — P + = arrot

See how easy it is? Let's do more.

Butterfly — B + = utterfly

Snake − S + 🐍 = 🐍nake

Camel − m + 🐫 = Ca🐫el

Giraffe − ff + 🦒 = Gira🦒e

Want to make your own? It's best if you start with simple words.

🌳ree   d🐶g   c☕p

Then try more complicated words and pictures. Here's Ellie's grand finale:

And, of course, her name:

McDdle

An Interview with the Author

Admit it—you were just like Ellie as a girl, weren't you?

Well . . .

Some of Ellie's adventures really happened to me. I loved to read a lot, write stories, draw, and make cartoons.

No fair!

I always have to be it!

I QUIT!

I loved games and word fun. But I didn't like being "it."
Okay, so I wasn't always the best team player.

I started keeping an almost-daily sketch journal when I was fifteen. A beloved teacher gave me a blank book to start in. I drew a lot and was usually dissatisfied with what I drew. But I kept trying to do my best.

The people around me—now and when I was young—are the inspiration for the cast of characters in my Ellie books.

"Ellie Math":

What was your favorite part of creating Ellie's story?

There were two favorite parts:
1) The affirmation I felt when my agent and some very respected editors said they loved the book.

2) Working on revisions.

I spent many, many days reworking the art and text. I racked my brain trying to make the book better, and I listened nonstop to reruns of my favorite funny TV shows. It was very hard work, but I loved every minute of it!

What advice do you have for young people wanting to become artists or writers?

Read, read, read. Anything you can get your hands on.

Draw, draw, draw. Don't get discouraged.

Open your brain to new activities, new sights, and new experiences. It'll give you something to write about.

Keep a journal, any kind.

Show your work to people you trust— teachers, librarians . . . they can help you find resources.

Be yourself. The world doesn't need more copies of things. It needs more YOU.

RUTH McNALLY BARSHAW, lifelong cartoonist, writer, and artist, worked in the advertising field, illustrated for newspapers, and won numerous essay-writing contests before becoming the creator of the Ellie McDoodle Diaries. In her spare time she studies martial arts, plays harmonica, and travels—always with a sketch journal. She lives in Lansing, Michigan, with her creative, prank-loving family. See her work at www.ruthexpress.com.

A good doodle diary can help you survive a new school, a new pet, a new sport, and so much more!

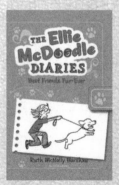